Stephen Chbosky's

The Perks of Being a Wallflower

BookCaps™ Study Guide
www.bookcaps.com

© 2012. All Rights Reserved.

Table of Contents

Historical Context

Stephen Chbosky was born in Pittsburg, Pennsylvania in 1970. He greatly enjoyed literature throughout his adolescence including the classics, horror novels, and fantasy. Some of his greatest influences came from J.D. Salinger, Tennessee Williams, and F. Scott Fitzgerald. Upon graduating from St. Clair High School in 1988 Chbosky attended the University of Southern California's screenwriting program, having been heavily influenced by Stewart Stern, screenwriter of "Rebel without a Cause". After graduating from college Chbowsky spent a lot of time writing screenplays, few of which would actually become movies, and also worked on a novel. While working on the novel, Chbowsky wrote the line "I guess that's just one of the perks of being a wallflower" and decided that the character he wanted to create was in that line. He scrapped the book and embarked on a new literary adventure that eventually became "The Perks of Being a Wallflower".

"The Perks of Being a Wallflower" was published in 1999 by MTV and immediately became popular with the adolescent crowd. There was some controversy surrounding the novel's portrayal of homosexuality, teen sexual activity, sexual and physical abuse, and drug use; however, Chbowsky felt that Charlie's adventures through his freshman year were true to the life of a teenager and somewhat autobiographical. Chbowsky has gone on to pen other novels as well as screenplays for movies as well as television shows and currently resides in Los Angeles, California. "The Perks of Being a Wallflower" is set to be released as a major motion picture in 2012.

Plot

Charlie is a fifteen-year-old who has just begun his freshman year in high school. He greatly misses his Aunt Helen, who passed away when he was seven, and he feels very lonely sometimes. Charlie narrates the novel by means of letters written to a Friend, whom he has never met but has heard of and thinks would be a good listener. He gets most of the joy in his life out of his advanced English class and the conversations about literature that he has with his teacher, Bill. Bill assigns Charlie many extra credit books to read and hopes that Charlie will learn a lot about himself and about life from the readings. Charlie becomes friends with a senior boy named Patrick, whom he finds out is having a secret homosexual relationship with a football player named Brad, and falls in love with Patrick's sister Sam. Charlie begins exploring the social scene that he never really feels a part of, drinking, experimenting with drugs, and smoking cigarettes. He has a falling out with Patrick and Sam when he kisses Sam rather than the girl he is dating during a game of Truth or Dare. Charlie is hesitant to fix his relationship with his friends until he jumps in to help Patrick in a fight against some football players, including Brad who, trying to keep his secret, called Patrick a "faggot". Charlie develops a deeper relationship than ever with both Patrick and Sam and learns some things about himself along the way that have caused him to be the wallflower that he is.

Characters

Charlie

Charlie is the fifteen-year-old narrator of the novel.
He narrates through a series of letters that he writes to
his "Friend", an older boy whom he has never
actually met but has heard about and thinks that he
would be a good listener. Charlie has lost a friend to
suicide and his favorite aunt to a car accident and
feels very alone, despite having a great family whom
he loves. Charlie loves literature and has a close
relationship with his English teacher, Bill, who
recommends books to Charlie that will help him
through the tough years of adolescence. Charlie has
experiences with sex, drugs, alcohol, homosexuality,
death, and physical and sexual abuse throughout
which he maintains maturity and understanding and
grows into a stronger person.

Sam

Sam is the sister of Patrick and Charlie's closest friend that is a girl. Charlie immediately falls in love with Sam and Sam loves Charlie as well, though in a different way. She is a nice girl who has a soft spot for Charlie and appreciates what a wonderful person he is. Sam dates a guy named Craig for the majority of the novel and Craig gets jealous when Charlie kisses Sam during a game of Truth or Dare, causing Sam to cut off ties with Charlie. After Sam and Charlie become friends again, Sam finds out that Craig had been cheating on her with multiple girls throughout their relationship. Sam and Charlie have a sexual encounter and agree to keep one another company via phone calls and letters when she goes away to Penn State for college.

Patrick

Patrick is the brother of Sam and is Charlie's best friend. Patrick is called "Nothing" by the kids in school, but Charlie refuses to call him this when he realizes what a good guy he is. When they first start hanging out, Charlie walks in on Patrick making out with a football player named Brad and Patrick is impressed by the mature and cool way that Charlie handles the situation. Patrick and Charlie have a falling out, but it is remedied when Charlie jumps in to help Patrick in a fight against some football players and they become closer than ever. Patrick goes through a depression and deep feeling of loneliness after his break up with Brad and Charlie stands by him through it all.

Bill

Bill is the teacher of Charlie's advanced English class. Bill has a great relationship with Charlie and enjoys speaking to Charlie about literature, even inviting him over to his home to do so. Bill thinks that Charlie is very smart and very special, which makes Charlie very emotional because the only other person to tell him that he is special was his Aunt Helen. Bill assigns Charlie various extra credit book to read throughout the school year, all of which teach Charlie about the trials and tribulations of adolescents and the various ways people deal with their problems. Charlie grows into a stronger person through his reading.

Brad

Brad is a football player and a closet homosexual, literally and figuratively as Charlie finds him making out with Patrick in a closet at a party. When Brad's father finds out about his relationship with Patrick, he beats him with a belt, and refuses to allow the relationship to happen, or to allow his son to be gay. Brad completely writes Patrick off and will not even acknowledge him at school. One day when Patrick tries to speak to him Brad yells "Faggot!" at him in the middle of the cafeteria which causes quite the brawl with Brad and the football players against Patrick and Charlie.

Mary Elizabeth

Mary Elizabeth is a girl whom Charlie dates, even though he likes Sam much more than he likes her. Mary Elizabeth asks Charlie to go to the Sadie Hawkins dance with her and talks incessantly about herself the entire time. Still, Charlie goes out with her again, and their date ends with a bit of sexual activity in her basement brought on by some brandy drinking. Charlie wants to break up with Mary Elizabeth but does not know how so when he is asked to "kiss the prettiest girl in the room" during a game of Truth or Dare he kisses Sam instead of Mary Elizabeth, making everyone uncomfortable.

Charlie's Sister

Charlie's sister is a senior in high school and at the start of the novel is dating a guy who Charlie sees as a bit of a pushover who cries too much. Charlie describes his sister as someone who is very mean to guys and thinks that her boyfriend is weak for putting up with it until the one day when he snaps and hits her. Charlie's sister does not break up with him but rather seems more attracted to him than ever before. She gets pregnant, and her boyfriend is furious, as he refuses to believe that it is his baby, and she has an abortion, which Charlie accompanies her to. Later, she begins to date a different guy named Erik, and, after graduation, she leaves to attend Sarah Lawrence for college.

Charlie's Brother

Charlie's brother is a star football player who is away at his freshman year of college throughout the novel. He plays football for Penn State and Charlie, and his family watch the team play in the Bowl on television. Charlie's brother is not very present in the novel, but Charlie mentions him from time to time, seemingly amazed and proud of how much his brother has changed and matured while he has been away at college. During a time when Charlie is feeling particularly lonely, his brother is able to come home for Christmas and to have a birthday dinner with Charlie, which makes him happy.

Craig

Craig is the guy that Sam is dating during the novel. Charlie is very upset when he finds out that Sam is dating Craig because he is in love with her though he has not told her. During a New Year's Eve party, Charlie already feels alone because Sam is there with Craig and Patrick is there with Brad, but then he hears Sam and Craig having sex and feels more alone than ever. Craig is jealous when Charlie kisses Sam, and this causes Sam to stop being friends with Charlie for a time. After prom, Sam learns that Craig had been cheating on her with multiple girls for the duration of their relationship, and she is devastated.

Bob

Bob is a guy who hosts most of the parties that Charlie and his friends attend. At the first party that Charlie goes to Bob offers him a brownie, which he is happy to accept, but does not tell Charlie that it is a pot brownie. Sam gets mad at Bob for getting Charlie high, but Charlie is not mad. In fact, he starts smoking pot and experimenting with other drugs regularly from that point on, and Bob becomes his dealer.

Aunt Helen

Aunt Helen is the sister of Charlie's mother and is Charlie's favorite aunt. On Charlie's seventh birthday, which happened to be Christmas Eve, Aunt Helen went to get Charlie a present and was involved in a bad car accident that killed her. Charlie was devastated by his aunt's death and often visits her grave to tell her about the things that are going on in his life. It is not until the end of Charlie's freshman year that his repressed memories come forward, and he realizes that he was sexually abused by Aunt Helen when they would watch television together on Saturday afternoons.

Charlie's Parents

Charlie's parents are described as being very hard-working, though his father works outside of the house and his mother works inside of the home. Charlie feels very lucky to have his parents as he feels they are very caring and fair, determined to not be as dysfunctional as their own families were when they were growing up. Charlie's parents are devastated when they learn that Charlie suffered sexual abuse at the hands of Aunt Helen, the sister of Charlie's mother, and Charlie's mother is particularly affected.

The Football Players

The football players are involved in the bullying of Patrick. When Brad is denying his homosexuality because of his father and acting out against Patrick, he calls him a faggot and starts a fight. The football players jump in to help Brad beat up Patrick, making the fight five against one until Charlie jumps in. Charlie uses moves he learned from his brother and really messes the football players up, saving Patrick from further beatings. Later, Brad quietly thanks Charlie for ending the fight.

Michael and Susan

Michael was a friend of Charlie, and he had committed suicide right before the start of the letters. Charlie is very upset at the death of Michael, more so than his fellow classmates. One time when Charlie is at the mall he sees Susan, the girlfriend of Michael, sitting with her friends. He goes up to her, to everyone's shock, and asks her if she misses Michael because he feels that he has to know. She does not answer him, and he walks away, hearing the others comment that he is a "freak," which he agrees with.

Charlie's Sister's Boyfriend

Charlie's sister's boyfriend at the start of the letters is someone who Charlie sees as very weak and too emotional for his sister. Charlie's sister is mean to guys, according to Charlie, and her boyfriend never stands up for himself against her. One day he snaps and hits her in the face, which rather than upset her seems to force her to have respect for him and their relationship only progresses and becomes more intense from there. When Charlie's sister gets pregnant, he gets very angry and breaks up with her, refusing to believe that the baby is his.

Themes

Loneliness

Loneliness a theme of adolescence which makes it central to this novel. Charlie experiences many of the same feelings of confusion and solitude that a lot of teenagers feel though he feels them in a slightly more complex way due to the sexual abuse in his pass and also the experience he has gained from reading literature. He feels like he is lucky to be surrounded by the people he has in his life but at the same time he feels as though he does not entirely fit in with anyone, except with his teacher Bill because they speak about the one thing that serves as an escape for Charlie: literature.

Sexuality

Sexuality is also a huge part of adolescence because it is a time when teenagers go through puberty and begin to explore their bodies and become interested sexually in others. Sexuality is explored from many viewpoints within in this novel: male/female sexual activity, male/male relationships, teen pregnancy and abortion, and sexual abuse. It is through sexual experience that Charlie's repressed memories of the sexual abuse he suffered at the hands of his favorite aunt come to light. Charlie is very wise and understanding about having a same-sex kiss with Patrick and also about his Aunt Helen's actions, but seems greatly uncomfortable with being sexually intimate with both Mary Elizabeth, as well as Sam.

Friendship

Friendship is something that becomes very comfortable to Charlie and at the same time seems quite foreign to him. When he enters high school he has no friends, as his only friend has just committed suicide. He decides to choose a guy that everyone else picks on to be his friend and holds on to that friendship with all that he has, even throughout a time of turmoil. Despite the fact that Patrick has basically written him off as a friend, Charlie comes to his aid when he is involved in a five-on-one fight with some football players. Patrick learns that Charlie's friendship is a very true, loyal, and valuable thing to have.

Compassion

Charlie is a very compassionate person. He feels very strongly, and his feelings go straight to his core. Possibly because of all of the literature that Charlie reads, and also due to all the conversations he has with psychiatrists, Charlie is very intuitive, wise, and understanding about all situations that present themselves in his life. He wants very much to be accepted and loved by those he cares about and tries his best to support them in any situation, as is illustrated when he accompanies his sister when she gets an abortion and also when he goes with Patrick to look for guys.

Understanding

Charlie seems to understand everything that other people are going through, but very little of what he is going through himself. The only person who really seems to understand what Charlie is going through is Bill, who recommends books based on those that he thinks will help Charlie to grow as a person. While many straight guys would be slightly taken aback if a friend of the same sex kissed them, Charlie understands that Patrick has a need for affection and intimacy and stands by him. Also, Charlie is not angry with his Aunt Helen when he realizes that he was sexually abused by her because he knows that she was dealing with a lot of demons in her life and understands that she was in pain.

Growth

Charlie grows tremendously as a person during his freshman year of high school and in the summer after. He begins as a boy who is depressed about just losing his friend to suicide and confused about where he belongs in the social world of his school. He feels lucky to be surrounded by his family and to find a couple of friends whom he is happy to spend time with and truly loves. It is not until after Charlie has a falling out with Patrick, Sam, and Mary Elizabeth and spends some time alone reflecting on his life that he truly begins to grow as a person. When Charlie realizes, after a sexual encounter with Sam, that he was molested as a child he truly makes a leap toward self-realization and vows to become a stronger and more active personality.

Fear

The major fear in this novel is of solitude. Charlie is not the only person who experiences this fear, Patrick and Sam experience it, as well. After the death of Michael and of his Aunt Helen, Charlie struggles to find a place where he feels like he belongs and people that he feels close to. When Brad is forced to break up with Patrick and then refuses to acknowledge him Patrick goes through a depression that leads him on a frantic search for another guy to be close to; he even kisses Charlie out of the need for intimacy. Sam even admits to Charlie when she is about to leave for school that she is worried about the loneliness she will feel away from everyone she loves.

Adolescence

Adolescence is central to the novel because it is about adolescents. Charlie experiences the same things that other adolescents do loneliness, drug and alcohol experimentation, sexual activity, school stressors, dysfunctional family gatherings, and unexpected death. He is wise enough to listen to what others have to say and to learn from the things that he experiences in life. Adolescence is a tough and confusing time for all of the teenage characters in the novel including Patrick, Sam, Charlie's sister, and Mary Elizabeth. They all grow from their experiences, which is a part of adolescence.

Maturity

Despite the obstacles that Charlie faces as a teenager and the experiences that he has gone through in his life, he manages to be mature beyond his years. Charlie has faced some things that, thankfully, not many teenager must face with the suicide of a friend and sexual abuse at the hands of a family member; he manages to keep a level-head and try to understand these experiences rather than be angry or sad about them. Charlie accepts other people for who they are and uses his experiences with them to learn more about himself. The mature and supportive way in which Charlie handles his relationship with Patrick, especially through Patrick's breakup, really show who he is as a person.

Depression

Charlie admits that he is depressed at the beginning of his letters. His friend has just committed suicide, and he lost his favorite aunt to a horrific car accident eight years prior. Charlie goes into a deep depression and a feeling of solitude every year around Christmas time due to his aunt's death for which he has received psychiatric counseling for a long time. Charlie also admits that when his friends do not call or go away on vacation he feels very alone and sad. Depression is something that many adolescents face and Charlie and his friends are no different.

Chapter Summary

Part One

It is Charlie's first year of high school, and he writes a letter to his "Friend", whom he has never met and is a bit older than him. Charlie's friend Michael has just taken his own life, and Charlie is much more upset about it than the other students in his grade. Charlie is youngest of three children in his family; he is fifteen. Charlie's older brother is a great football player and is going to play for Penn State. His older sister is, according to Charlie, mean to guys. Both of Charlie's parents are very hard-working but in different ways; his father works hard out of the home, and his mother works hard within the home. Charlie is very fond of his Aunt Helen, his mother's sister, who has passed away. Aunt Helen had lived with Charlie and his family for a few years after she went through a bad time in her life.

The following day will be Charlie's very first day of high school, and he is terrified and nervous. Charlie is picked on a lot in school and it makes the whole experience pretty awful for him. He learned some moves from his brother to defend himself, but when he uses the moves on the boy who is picking on him, the boy actually gets hurt. Charlie is very effected by the fact that he hurt the other boy and breaks down emotionally, crying, because all he was trying to do is defend himself not to cause the other boy pain. The part of school that Charlie does enjoy is his advanced English class. His teacher, who tells Charlie to call him Bill when they are not in class, gives him "To Kill a Mockingbird" to read as extra credit. Charlie does not need extra credit but gets the assignment because he is ahead of the other students and doing very well.

Charlie's sister's current boyfriend is pretty weak in Charlie's opinion. The boy makes her mixed tapes and is very emotional; he even cries sometimes. One day after Charlie's sister is especially cruel to her boyfriend he loses control and hits her in the face. She has absolutely no reaction to being hit in the face, but she must have been impressed with his ability to stand up for himself because from that moment on they are officially a couple. Charlie does not say anything about seeing him hit her, nor does he say anything about seeing them both naked on the couch together.

Charlie does not only enjoy his English class, but he enjoys Shop class, as well. One of the other students in his class is named Nothing. Nothing is not his real name but one day when the other students were teasing him and calling him Patty instead of Patrick he told them to call him his real name or call him nothing; they decided to call him Nothing. Charlie thinks about when he visited the place where Aunt Helen is buried. He also thinks about his family, watching the last episode of M.A.S.H. with them, and how great he thinks they are. He even appreciates the fact that his father is not afraid to cry, though he does try to hide it.

Charlie goes to a football game, and he sees Nothing; he knows that Nothing will talk to him regardless of the fact that Charlie is younger because Nothing is a

friendly guy. Nothing introduces himself to Charlie
using his birth name, Patrick. He also introduces
Charlie to the girl that he is hanging out with, Sam,
who is very good looking. After the game, Patrick
invites Charlie to go to the Big Boy with him, and
Sam and Charlie decides that he will call Patrick by
his real name because he is a nice guy. Charlie also
finds himself having quite the crush on Sam. Charlie
finds out that Sam is not Patrick's girlfriend but is his
sister; he then decides that he wants to ask Sam to go
out with him sometime. When Charlie has a sexual
dream about Sam, he wakes up embarrassed about it
and decides that he would like to have her as just a
friend rather than as a girlfriend.

One day after school Charlie hangs out to talk with
Bill about life and about girls. He decides to tell Bill
about his sister and boyfriend because Bill does not
know then and, therefore, cannot judge. Bill only tells
Charlie that "we accept the love we think we
deserve". Charlie walks home from school that day,
and when he gets home he sees his parents outside
with his sister, who is crying. Apparently Bill had
called Charlie's parents, and told them that his sister's
boyfriend hit her, and, in turn, they forbid her from
dating someone who is abusive. Charlie's sister tells
him that she hates him. Charlie's father does not hit
the children, except one time when he did it and
immediately apologized; his stepfather had been
abusive and he always swore that he would not do the
same with his own kids. Charlie's father talked to the
boyfriend's parents, and the relationship seemed to be
over. Charlie knows he did the right thing, and his

father agrees, but his sister is still very angry with him.

Charlie is given another extra credit assignment by Bill; this time it is "Peter Pan", which Charlie enjoys very much. Bill had suggested to Charlie that he be a more active participant in life rather than just being an observer and Charlie was trying to love up to that advice. Charlie goes to a party after Homecoming with Patrick and Sam where everyone is older than him. When Charlie is offered beer, he refuses because he tried one when he was twelve and he was not a fan. When Charlie finds himself away from Patrick and Sam, he is offered a brownie from Bob, the host of the party, unaware that they are pot brownies, and soon he is high. Sam is furious when she finds out and she makes Charlie a milkshake. Charlie goes to the bathroom and explores noises he hears coming from a closet; he finds Patrick and a football player named Brad making out. Brad is freaked out, but Patrick assures him that Charlie will keep quiet about the situation because he is a wallflower. Patrick tells Charlie later that Charlie sees things and says nothing because he understands. That night was Charlie's first party and will certainly be unforgettable.

Part Two

Charlie is trying to think of Sam as just a friend, but he is unsuccessful; he feels like he is in love with her. Charlie sees his feelings for Sam as real, pure, and respectful; this is much different than the way he sees her new boyfriend Craig's feelings for her. He thinks that Craig has very little respect for Sam and when Charlie asks his sister about it she says that Sam just has low self-esteem. She talks to Charlie about her boyfriend, whom she is still seeing secretly, and their meetings together when they sneak out at night. She thinks that they will get married someday. Charlie is concerned, but she insists that he does not hit her anymore.

Charlie's brother is supposed to come home for Thanksgiving which is coming up soon, but he is falling behind on schoolwork because of football and will be unable to make it. Charlie's mother is very upset that he cannot make it. The family has Thanksgiving dinner with Charlie's mother's family, and Charlie admits that it goes much smoother than past holidays have gone; usually there is a lot of drunken fighting and some tears. Christmas is coming up soon and Sam organizes the Secret Santa that she does every year. Charlie hopes that he will draw Sam's name but instead he draws Patrick's. Charlie decides to give Patrick a mixed tape that he made him with songs on it that will remind Patrick that he belongs somewhere even when he is feeling like he doesn't. For Charlie's gifts, he receives socks, a belt, a tie, pants, and shoes; he is sure that most of them are from a thrift store. There is a note telling him to wear the outfit to a party at Sam's house where the Secret Santas will be revealed.

At the party, Charlie is the youngest again. Patrick comes in and reveals himself as Charlie's gift-giver, toting a jacket to match the rest of Charlie's outfit. Patrick tells Charlie that a proper author should have a proper suit. Charlie gives Patrick a poem and reads it aloud; everyone loves the poem. Charlie agrees that it is beautiful, despite the fact that it is a suicide note. Charlie and Sam exchange gifts with one another as well; Charlie gives Sam a record that belonged to Aunt Helen and Sam gives Charlie a used typewriter that she wants him to use to write about her. Sam tells Charlie she loves him, and she kisses him; as happy as he is he knows that, she loves him as a friend. Sam tells Charlie that she wanted his first kiss to be from a person who loves him. Bill gave Charlie some more books to read outside of the class assignments, including "The Great Gatsby", "A Separate Peace", and "Catcher in the Rye", which he is reading over his Christmas break.

Sam and Patrick go with their family to the Grand Canyon for Christmas and Charlie feels very lonely without them. Charlie begins to have feelings of depression like he experienced before he had friends, but he feels better when he remembers things that make him happy, like the kiss from Sam. Charlie always feels sort of depressed around the holidays. He hopes that Patrick and Sam will call him for his birthday, which is on Christmas Eve. Charlie is disappointed when they do not call him, but he is happy that his brother was able to come home from college, and he has a nice birthday dinner with his family. For Christmas Day Charlie's family visits with his father's side in Ohio. His father's side of the family is a lot like his mother's side of the family, there is some alcohol abuse and physical abuse as well as a general feeling of unease.

Charlie's Aunt Helen had been molested by a friend of her family. Following the abuse Helen had become an addict and found herself in a series of relationships with men who were abusive to her. After a while, she came to live with Charlie and his family to get her life back on track. Aunt Helen left to get Charlie a present on the day of his seventh birthday, and she was involved in a horrible car accident that killed her. Charlie felt like Aunt Helen's death was his fault because she was buying a present for his birthday; he had to see doctors for a long time because he was very distraught. Every year since Aunt Helen's death Charlie gets very depressed around the Christmas holidays. The first thing that Charlie does when he is able to drive is to visit the place where Aunt Helen is buried. He tells her everything that he can think of and promises her that he will not cry unless it is a moment that calls for it, rather than just when he is upset.

Charlie goes to a New Year's Eve party where he feels very alone. Sam is there with Craig and Patrick is there with Brad; Charlie has no one. Charlie decides to get high again, and he becomes increasingly depressed, especially when he hears Sam having sex with Craig. Charlie feels like he finally understands the last line of the suicide poem that he gave to Patrick though he insists to his Friend that he never really wanted to kill himself.

Part Three

January 4, 1992 Charlie writes a letter to his Friend apologizing for the previous letter. He says that he blacked out for much of the New Year's Eve party, and he was found lying outside in the snow by some policemen. He had turned blue and was sleeping so he was taken to the emergency room. His parents are not surprised by this behavior as they find it to be relatively normal for him, as do the emergency room staff. They do not think that Charlie's attendance of the party had anything to do with his condition, and he refuses to tell them that he took LSD, though he promises himself he will not ever take it again. His family watches the Penn State football game together; they are playing in the Bowl. He tries to have some time with his family , and they try to make a connection with him, but with little success. Days after Charlie's experience he is still feeling effects from the LSD and he gets scared that the effects will never go away. Sam and Patrick tell him that the effects will go away, and he feels slightly better, but he starts smoking cigarettes that day and is soon up to smoking ten per day. Charlie does not want to think about life, so he just keeps reading "Catcher in the Rye" over and over again. His psychiatrist is one of the only people he speaks to about the things that confuse him.

Charlie receives two more books from Bill, "On the Road" and "Naked Lunch". His school is putting on a production of the Rocky Horror Picture Show and Charlie gladly accepts the role of Rocky. When the Sadie Hawkins Dance rolls around, a girl named

Mary Elizabeth asks Charlie to go with her, and he accepts. At the dance, Mary Elizabeth does not stop talking about herself and Sam is feeling very lonely. Patrick goes out to the parking lot to get high with the school counselor and Charlie's sister and her boyfriend get into a big fight. At home that night Charlie tries to comfort his sister and learns that she is pregnant; the reason her boyfriend was arguing with her is because he does not think the baby is his.

Charlie's sister is going to have an abortion that week, and Charlie agrees to go with her for moral support. Inside the clinic, Charlie panics and cries; he decides to wait outside in the car, so no one calls their parents. Charlie's sister comes out later and naps for a little while before they go back home. She decides that she is going to tell her boyfriend that it was a false alarm, and she was not really pregnant.

Charlie goes on another date with Mary Elizabeth. At the end, of the date they go down to Mary Elizabeth's basement and have some brandy, which leads to Charlie's first sexual encounter. Everyone is happy about Charlie's sexual experience except for him; Mary Elizabeth gets extremely clingy and her incessant need to talk all the time is really starting to get on his nerves. Charlie considers breaking things off with Mary Elizabeth for over a week when they end up playing Truth or Dare at a party with a bunch of other people. Charlie refuses to choose "truth" because he does not want anyone to ask him any questions about Mary Elizabeth. The fallout happens when Patrick dares Charlie to kiss the prettiest girl who is in the room and rather than kiss Mary

Elizabeth Charlie kisses Sam. As soon as it happens it is over as Patrick is rushing Charlie out the door and bringing him home. Over the next week, no one calls Charlie, and he spends his time reading "Hamlet", which is his latest recommendation from Bill. He feels comfort in reading "Hamlet" because the characters remind him that he is not the only person who feels isolated and lonely. Charlie and Mary Elizabeth are officially over, just as he wanted, but so is his relationship with Patrick and Sam which he did not want. Craig was jealous when Charlie kissed Sam, so Sam decided that she did not want to see Charlie anymore; every time Charlie tries to hang out with Patrick, he has something else to do. Charlie is so lonely that he does not know what to do. He decides to go visit his Aunt Helen and tell her everything that is going on it his life, but it does not work as well as it always did before. Charlie calls Bob to buy some pot, as he smokes it regularly now.

Part Four

At school, no one wants to speak to Charlie anymore. Charlie does not have anyone whom he socializes with; in fact the only person who he speaks to is his psychiatrist. In his free time, Charlie goes to the mall and people watches; he wonders what makes people want to hang out at the mall. One day while Charlie is watching people at the mall he sees a little boy who cannot find his mother and then sees them reunite; he also sees a girl named Susan who was the girlfriend of Michael before he killed himself. Charlie walks up to the table that Susan and her friends are sitting at, and they all stare at him in silence. He cannot help himself from asking Susan whether or not she misses Michael; she does not answer him, and as he walks away the people at her table remark that he is a "freak". Charlie cannot help himself but to agree with them.

One day when Charlie is at Bob's house buying pot, he hears that Brad's father discovered Brad's relationship with Patrick, and he beat Brad with his belt. No one has seen Brad for a week now. Charlie wants to call Patrick and see if he is okay and if Brad is okay, but he knows that his phone calls are not welcome anymore. Instead of calling Charlie goes to see the Rocky Horror Picture Show where he knows Patrick, Sam, and Mary Elizabeth are performing; he is relieved to see that they are all there, and they are all okay. When Charlie gets home, he sees that his sister is there with Erik, her new boyfriend. He retreats to his room to read his latest book from Bill, "The Stranger".

Things begin to change back at school. Brad has returned, but he will not speak to Patrick no matter how many times Patrick tries. There are a few times when Charlie notices that Patrick is crying outside of the school, and he wishes he could console him, but he knows that Patrick does not want to speak to him. At lunch one day, Patrick walks up to Brad where he is sitting with his football friends and tries to speak to him quietly. Brad will not speak to Patrick, and when Patrick walks away Brad yells "Faggot!" after him. Patrick turns back toward Brad and asks him what he said; Brad repeats himself. Patrick lunges at Brad and hits him. Not only does Brad fight back but some of his teammates jump in as well; soon the fight is five football players against Patrick. Charlie cannot stand to see Patrick being beaten up on like this and he jumps in, using some of the moves that he learned from his brother. Charlie causes some serious damage in the fight and soon the guys start to back off, including Brad. Charlie sees how beaten up Patrick is and tells Brad that if he ever acts in such a way again then he will tell the whole school everything that he knows. Brad and Charlie are the only ones who are not suspended, though they each much serve detention for a month. The first day that Charlie and Brad share detention Brad thanks Charlie for stepping in and ending the fight; though he does so quietly so no one else hears. There is no other contact between the two of them for the rest of their detentions. After detention that day Charlie finds that Sam is waiting for him and things seem to have gone back to almost the way they were before the kiss. Charlie learns that

Mary Elizabeth is seeing an older guy now and that Patrick is never happy anymore, he has even given up his role in Rocky Horror Picture Show.

Patrick and Charlie begin to spend time together again though the time mostly consists of Charlie listening to Patrick being bitter and morose. One day after the boys spend time reminiscing about the fun times they have had and laughing together Patrick kisses Charlie. Charlie does not get mad at Patrick but rather understands his need for affection. When Patrick apologizes and starts crying about Brad and how much he misses him Charlie understands that need, as well. Patrick and Charlie get drunk together often from that point on, and Patrick takes Charlie to the places that he knows men go to meet other men. Charlie is happy to accompany his friend and is patient for Patrick to find whatever it is that he is looking for; he is also supportive when Patrick does not find it time and time again. One night they see Brad and Brad does not even notice them; this is the night when Patrick stops his drinking habit.

Charlie's psychiatrist starts to ask him strange questions about the earlier years in his life. In school Bill has given him "Fountainhead" as his final book to read and encourages him to filter the information in the novel rather than to take it all in. The school year is coming to an end, and Charlie feels sure that he will have straight A's that year. Patrick will be graduating soon, and has decided that he will go to the University of Washington, so he can be close to the music scene that he is so drawn to. Sam will be going to Penn State, Charlie's sister will go to Sarah Lawrence, and Mary Elizabeth will be going to Berkeley. Charlie is happy that Sam will be going to Penn State because that means he can visit his brother and Sam at the same time.

Charlie feels very lonely after the seniors leave the school and he is happy to know that prom night seems to have gone well for all of them. Unfortunately, the day after prom Sam learns that Craig had been cheating on her with multiple girls and throughout their entire relationship. Sam is devastated and despite the fact that Charlie thought he would be happy when they broke up he is sad for Sam and does not like to see her so upset. Charlie realizes that the fact that he is hurting because a person he loves is hurting is what real love is all about. Bill asks Charlie over to his house one day, and Charlie happily agrees; he enjoys his discusses of literature with Bill and his girlfriend. Charlie is flattered and happy when Bill tells him that he is special because his Aunt Helen was the last person who told him that.

When graduation day comes, Charlie is glad to see his brother home from school and matured from a year away. His family goes to the ceremony and watches his sister give her speech as Salutatorian and Charlie watches his friends all receive their diplomas. Charlie's family is all gathered together at his house later celebrating when Sam calls and asks him to come over and celebrate with them. As soon as Charlie's relatives leave he heads over to Sam and Patrick's house and brings them the gifts he got.

Charlie's friends love his presents and how thoughtful he is, and Sam tells Charlie, when he starts to cry, that she is as scared of going away to school as he is to be alone in the high school in the fall. Sam and Charlie agree that they will write one another, and call all the time, so they do not get too lonely.

Everyone gets together for one last hoorah the night before Sam goes away to school. As the night is ending, Charlie finds himself and Sam alone in her room. Sam tells Charlie that he needs to learn to act out of what he wants rather than what others want rather than being so passive about his own life. Charlie kisses Sam and soon the kiss leads to the two of them getting sexual. Just when they are really getting into things Charlie tells Sam that he needs to stop; he lets Sam believe it is because he is not ready, but he feels like there is more to it than that. That night Charlie has a dream that he was having sex with Aunt Helen and when he wakes he has a staggering feeling that what he dreamed had actually happened at some point. Sam leaves for college and Charlie ends his letter to his Friend, thanking him for listening to a random kid who is sending him letters. Charlie does not even know the Friend, he is merely a person that Charlie heard about in conversation; but he feels sure that a person who does not always try to sleep with girls even though he can is probably a good listener. Charlie thanks his Friend and wishes him a good life.

Epilogue

Charlie spends the two months of summer after his freshman year in the hospital. He remembers mailing the letters to his Friend, but he does not remember much else. The event that led to him being placed in the hospital was when Charlie's mother found him watching television while lying naked on the couch. Over the course of his visits with doctors and psychiatrists, Charlie has become absolutely sure that his Aunt Helen would molest him while they watched television together on Saturday afternoons. Charlie has learned that neither his brother nor his sister had experienced the same thing with Aunt Helen, but they feel horrible for what he went through. Charlie's mother is absolutely horrified at the way her sister acted toward Charlie, but Charlie does not blame Aunt Helen. He knows that she had many demons in her life that caused her to act a certain way. Charlie begins to feel much stronger as his friends and family come to visit and he writes one more letter to his Friend. He tells him that he is ready to enter school and is no longer afraid of being alone. He vows to participate in more things this year and try to make friends; since he will be so busy he will probably not be able to write any more letters, which he apologizes for. Charlie tells his Friend that if this ends up as the final letter to always know that he is doing well and if he isn't then he will be soon, and he hopes the same for his Friend.

About BookCaps

We all need refreshers every now and then. Whether you are a student trying to cram for that big final, or someone just trying to understand a book more, BookCaps can help. We are a small, but growing company, and are adding titles every month.

Visit www.bookcaps.com to see more of our books, or contact us with any questions.

Cover Image © Richard Laschon - Fotolia.com

Printed in Great Britain
by Amazon.co.uk, Ltd.,
Marston Gate.